It's the coolest school in space!

Young Teggs Stegosaur is a pupil at
Astrosaurs ACADEMY – where dinosaurs
train to be space-exploring **Astrosaurs**.
With his best friends Blink and Dutch
beside him, amazing adventures and
far-out fun are never far away!

For more astro-fun visit the website
www.astrosaursacademy.co.uk

Astrosaurs ACADEMY

STEVE COLE

DEADLY DRAMA!

Illustrated by Woody Fox

RED FOX

DEADLY DRAMA!
A RED FOX BOOK 978 1 862 30885 5

First published in Great Britain by Red Fox,
an imprint of Random House Children's Books
A Random House Group Company

This edition published 2009

1 3 5 7 9 10 8 6 4 2

The Random House Group Limited supports the Forest Stewardship
Council (FSC), the leading international forest certification
organization. All our titles that are printed on Greenpeace-approved
FSC-certified paper carry the FSC logo. Our paper procurement policy
can be found at www.rbooks.co.uk/environment.

Set in16/20pt Bembo Schoolbook by
Falcon Oast Graphic Art Ltd

Red Fox Books are published by Random House Children's Books,
61–63 Uxbridge Road, London W5 5SA

www.kidsatrandomhouse.co.uk
www.rbooks.co.uk

Addresses for companies within The Random House Group Limited can
be found at: www.randomhouse.co.uk/offices.htm

THE RANDOM HOUSE GROUP Limited Reg. No. 954009

A CIP catalogue record for this book is available from
the British Library.

Printed in the UK by CPI Bookmarque, Croydon, CR0 4TD

For Chris Newton and
Jasmine Fassl — thanks for everything!

WELCOME TO THE COOLEST SCHOOL IN SPACE . . .

Most people think that dinosaurs are extinct. Most people believe that these weird and wondrous reptiles were wiped out when a massive space rock smashed into the Earth, 65 million years ago.

HA! What do *they* know? The dinosaurs were way cleverer than anyone thought . . .

This is what *really* happened: they saw that big lump of space rock coming, and when it became clear that dino-life could not survive such a terrible crash, the dinosaurs all took off in huge, dung-powered spaceships before the rock hit.

They set their sights on the stars and left the Earth, never to return . . .

Now, 65 million years later, both plant-eaters and meat-eaters have built massive empires in space. But the carnivores are never happy unless  they're causing trouble. That's why the Dinosaur Space Service needs herbivore heroes to defend the Vegetarian Sector. Such heroes have a special name. They are called ASTROSAURS.

But you can't change from a dinosaur to an astrosaur overnight. It takes years of training on the special planet of Astro Prime in a *very* special place . . . the Astrosaurs Academy! It's a sensational

space school where
manic missions
and incredible
adventures are
the only
subjects! The
academy's doors
are always open,
but only to the
bravest, boldest
dinosaurs . . .

And to YOU!

*NOTE: One of the most famous astrosaurs of
all is Captain Teggs Stegosaur. This
staggering stegosaurus is the star of many
stories . . . But before he became a spaceship
captain, he was a cadet at Astrosaurs
Academy. These are the adventures of the
young Teggs and his friends – adventures
that made him the dinosaur he is today!*

Talking Dinosaur!

How to say the prehistoric names in
DEADLY DRAMA!

STEGOSAURUS – *STEG-oh-SORE-us*

DIPLODOCUS – *di-PLOH-de-kus*

DICERATOPS – *dye-SERRA-tops*

ANKYLOSAUR – *an-KILE-oh-SORE*

DRYOSAURUS – *DRY-oh-SORE-us*

VULCANODON – *vul-CAN-oh-don*

BAGACERATOPS – *bag-uh-SERRA-tops*

PTERODACTYL – *teh-roh-DAK-til*

PTEROSAUR – *teh-roh-SORE*

The cadets

THE DARING DINOS

Teggs

Dutch

Blink

DAMONA'S DARLINGS

Damona

Netta

Splatt

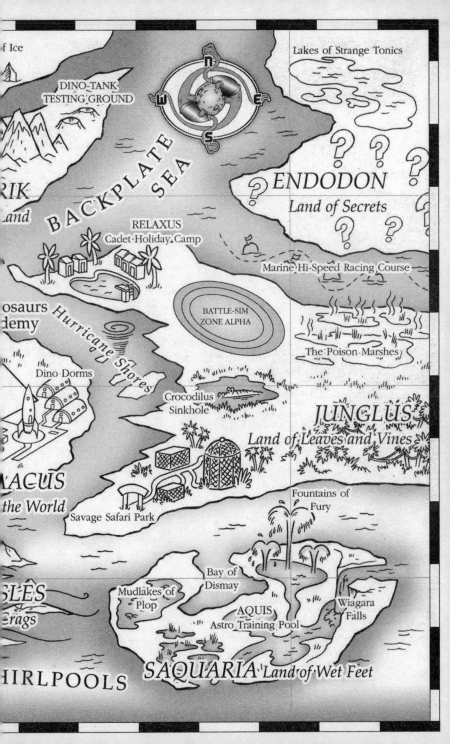

Chapter One

AWESOME AUDITION

Teggs Stegosaur
was trying to stop
his knees knocking.

In his time
at Astrosaurs
Academy – the
sensational school
where dinosaurs
trained for
adventures in outer
space – Teggs had faced all
kinds of baddies, from terrifying T. rexes
to rotten raptors. But he had never felt
more frightened than he did now . . .

He turned to his best friends, Blink and

Dutch, and shook his head. "Why did we ever say we'd do this dumb audition?"

"It seemed a good idea at the time, dude. But now, I'm petrified!" Dutch, a stocky green diplodocus, clutched his tummy. "Never mind butterflies in the stomach, I think I've got a flock of dino-birds in there!"

"Oi!" squawked Blink, who was a dino-bird himself. Then he smiled and flapped his yellow, leathery wings. "I'm really looking forward to our audition. Just imagine if we all end up in a real movie! Millions of plant-eaters will see it, all across the Vegetarian Sector!"

Teggs groaned again. "Don't, Blink — I can feel some serious stage fright coming on!"

Just a week ago, the Academy's head — Commander Gruff — had been approached by famous film director Stefano Spielsaur. The movie-maker wanted to shoot a dramatic documentary on how dino-cadets trained to be astrosaurs! Thinking it would encourage more brilliant young dinosaurs to join the Space Service, Gruff had agreed. And now the hunt was on for the lucky cadets who would star in the film . . .

"I just know you'll be brilliant, guys," said Blink kindly as they waited their turn. "Remember, Gruff said Mr Spielsaur is looking for dinosaurs who grab every chance for adventure and action that comes their way and who

work well as a team." He hopped
between his friends and peered up at
them through his chunky specs. "Sound
familiar?"

"It's us!" Teggs brightened a little.
"We're the Daring Dinos, we live for
adventure and action – and we work
brilliantly as a team!"

"But so many other cadets have
turned up." Dutch gestured to the row of
blue-uniformed dinosaurs snaking down
the corridor. "Gruff said only three
teams will be chosen to take part . . ."

"Well, the first
team's been picked
already!" A pretty
red diceratops burst
through the doors
from the main hall,
smiling smugly.
"Make way, make
way – Damona Furst
is going to be a star!"

4

"Star?" Dutch grimaced. "A black hole, more like!"

"Well done, Damona," said Teggs politely. Damona was brave and bright but very annoying – and his biggest rival. "What did you have to do?"

"Nothing much." Damona shrugged. "Stef obviously just loves us!"

Blink looked blank. "Stef?"

"Stef Spielsaur, the director, of course!" Damona peered back into the hall and frowned. "Netta, Splatt, come on!"

"What are they doing?" asked Teggs.

"They're wearing their new movie-star dark glasses," Damona explained. "So dark that they can't quite find their way out!"

Netta was a pink ankylosaur and Splatt was a green, super-speedy dryosaurus. Teggs grinned as the posing pair stumbled out of the hall and almost tripped over Damona's tail!

"How about that?" trilled Netta. "Damona's Darlings are going to be famous!"

"*And* we miss a week's lessons while we're filming!" said Splatt. He snootily offered Dutch a piece of paper with a scribble on. "I suppose you'd like my autograph, right?"

"Thanks, dude," said Dutch with a wicked smile. "How did you guess I'd run out of toilet paper?"

Splatt pulled off his shades and scowled – but the next moment, a commanding voice echoed out from inside the hall. "NEXT!"

"That's us!" Blink held out his clawed hand. "Do we dare to audition for Stefano Spielsaur's mega-movie?"

Teggs and Dutch grinned and placed their hands on top of his. "WE DARE!"

"Good luck, boys!" Damona called as the three friends hurried into the hall. "Try not to be too rubbish!"

Teggs felt his legs wobble as he approached the stage set up at the front of the large, pyramid-shaped room. Then he saw a white vulcanodon perched on a canvas chair, surrounded by assistants, and gulped loudly. It could only be Stefano Spielsaur!

The director looked at Teggs and his friends. "Who are you?"

"Blink, Teggs and Dutch," said Blink eagerly as he led the way onto the stage. "We're the Daring Dinos."

"Aha," said Spielsaur, making notes on a clipboard.

"We can't wait to show everyone how cool it is at the Academy!" Blink added.

"We – we love it here," stammered Dutch.

"And we work really well as a bean," Teggs blurted. "Um – a *team*, I mean." He blushed red at his mistake.

Spielsaur frowned.

"Er . . . would you like to see us in action, sir?" Blink called. "We do this cool trick where Teggs and Dutch launch me like a missile and—"

"I've seen enough," said Spielsaur. "And, you know what? You're in the movie!"

Dutch sprang into the air, and Teggs almost fell over with shock. "WOW!"

Blink
yelled,
whizzing
about like a
parrot who'd just
sat on a firecracker.

"Calm down," Spielsaur
snapped. "This is a serious business. We
start filming tomorrow. An astro-jet will
leave here at seven to take you to the
marine high-speed racing course off the
coast of Junglus. Now, scram!"

"I don't believe it!" Blink staggered off
the stage with his friends in a daze.

"Me neither." Teggs frowned. "We
didn't even have to do anything!"

"Don't knock it, dude." Dutch grinned. "The important thing is, Damona's Darlings won't have all the fun — we're going to star in the film and be famous too. BRING IT ON!"

Chapter Two

JETTING TO DANGER

Early the next morning, nine very excited cadets headed for the wet and wild marine racing course.

Teggs sat with Dutch and Blink on board the astro-jet, finishing off a gigantic breakfast of ferns and berries. Blink had his face pressed up against a window, searching for the first sight of their destination.

Damona's Darlings were sprawled out in their dark glasses, sipping icy drinks and acting like film stars.

The other cadets on board were Ick, Wick and Honko, who made a team called the Baggy Brothers. They were bagaceratops triplets – stocky, enthusiastic and easy to like. Teggs was glad they were all sharing this unusual adventure together.

Ick was jumping up and down in his seat with excitement.

14

"Awesome week ahead, guys!"

"Totally," Wick agreed.

"And then some!" Honko added.

Suddenly, Blink gave a whoop. "I just glimpsed the Junglus coast!"

Teggs felt his tummy tingle. He and the others had been to Junglus once before on a particularly scale-raising adventure.

Damona shivered. "I hope no one tries to shoot us this time."

"Unless it's with a camera," Dutch said firmly.

"Chill-out-a-saurus!" Wick told them. "We're making a movie with an A-list director! What could possibly go wrong?"

Flying taxis – large carriages pulled by pterodactyls – pulled up just as the

astro-jet landed on a sandy beach. The
cadets hopped in and the taxis took off.
As Teggs gazed out over the incredible
landscape of giant mossy cliffs and
churning orange water, he found Blink's
excitement was catching. He smiled
happily, looking forward to the
adventure ahead.

"Look!" Damona stood up in her taxi

and pointed. "There's the film crew!"

A few hundred metres ahead, three large silver trailers had been parked and lots of dinosaurs were milling about. A diplodocus held a microphone on a long stick. A woolly rhino was setting up a film camera.

And there, perched on his canvas chair, was Stefano Spielsaur.

"Come on, you cadets!" Spielsaur yelled as the taxis stopped beside the lorries. "We've got a movie to make!"

As Damona's Darlings and the Baggy Brothers hurried out of their taxis, Teggs gulped nervously. "Mr Spielsaur is a bit grumpy."

"He seems kind of stressed about something today," agreed the woolly rhino with the camera. "My name's Cammino, by the way – I'll be filming  you from ground level on this shoot, while Lenswing here handles the views from above."

"Squawk!" A small pterosaur hopped out from behind him, wearing a kind of crash helmet with a camera on top of it. She smiled shyly at Teggs, Dutch and Blink.

"She can't speak," Cammino explained. "But she's the sharpest-eyed camera-saur in the business!"

With a smile and a wave to the crew members, the Daring Dinos joined their fellow cadets at Spielsaur's side.

"Now, listen." The director pointed to three sleek, narrow, rocket-powered boats tied to a jetty in the surging sea. "This film will show everyone how much fun you cadets have at the Academy. So we will start by showing you racing around the course in jet-canoes."

Dutch surveyed the huge blue marker buoys bobbing in the choppy water and grinned. "Sounds fun to me, dude!"

"Awesome!" chorused the Baggy Brothers, and Teggs and Blink high-fived.

"What's my motivation for this scene?" asked Damona grandly.

"Your motivation is that I'll send you home if you ask such silly questions again!" Spielsaur hollered. "I make documentaries, not dramas. Now, go jump in your jet-canoe and have some fun . . ."

Splatt and Netta were already running off to the nearest jet-canoe, and Damona followed meekly, looking even redder than usual.

The triplets took the second jet-canoe, while Teggs and his friends took the third. The boats rocked wildly in the turbulent water as all the cadets pulled on chunky orange life jackets and started up the

engines. Cammino
fiddled with his
camera. Lenswing
launched herself
into the air and
circled above the
marker buoys.

"Now, I've chosen the most advanced
part of the marine racing course 'cause
it will look coolest on camera," Spielsaur
went on. "But remember, there's a coral
reef just half a mile north. It's so sharp
it can cut metal! I know the jet-canoes
are designed to be unsinkable – but in

case of trouble, I've got ultra-fast robot lifeguards standing by to fish you all out."

Teggs waited impatiently as nine chunky yellow robots filed from one of the trailers and lined up along the jetty. He couldn't wait to take the powerful jet-canoe out into the churning sea!

"When I shout 'Action!' just steer all around the buoys so we can film you from lots of angles," Spielsaur called. "Here goes . . . Lights! Camera! ACTION!"

"Yeee-hooooooooooo!" Dutch shouted as the Daring Dinos' jet-canoe zoomed away. Teggs laughed and held onto

Blink as the boat was tossed this way
and that by the foaming ocean. Splatt
was steering Damona's Darlings' canoe
in a wide circle, while Netta and
Damona posed in the back. The triplets
grinned and waved as they cut a zigzag
path through the water.

"Good!" Spielsaur yelled
encouragingly as the cadets zoomed
around. The diplodocus waved his
microphone and Lenswing swooped
gracefully overhead, filming all the
action. "Now, Cammino, go in for a
close-up on those triplets . . ."

But suddenly, the Baggy Brothers
shouted out in alarm.

"Our boat's sprung a leak," cried Wick.

Ick gulped. "The situation is sink-a-saurus!"

"And then some!" Honko added.

With horror, Teggs saw it was true – the triplets' jet-canoe was dipping under the raging waters.

"Lifeguards, quick!" Spielsaur shouted to the yellow robots. But, one by one, the nine mechanical lifeguards toppled into the tide like statues and sank to the bottom.

Dutch gasped. "They've gone wrong!"

"And the Baggy Brothers are going under!" Blink wailed as the helpless canoe was swept away by a massive wave. "If they hit that coral reef, they'll be doomed for sure!"

Chapter Three

ACTION AT THE REEF

"Quickly, Dutch, steer us towards the triplets!" Teggs shouted. "We have to rescue them."

Dutch was already on the case, sending the jet-canoe roaring through the water. Damona did the same, rocketing over the

waves in the Darlings'
boat. But the
sinking canoe was
spinning away
too quickly . . .

"It's no
good!" Dutch
shouted from the tiller.
"By the time we've caught them up,
they'll be on the reef!"

"It'll cut them to bits," said Teggs
grimly.

"Guys!" Blink exclaimed. "Remember
the trick we were going to do at our
audition?"

Dutch frowned. "How will launching
you like a missile help now, dude?"

"I'll show you." Blink flapped his
wings urgently. "Now, point me at the
triplets' canoe!"

Their boat bucked and rocked on the
stormy waves, and Teggs could barely
keep his balance as he and Dutch got

into position. Then they linked tails and
Blink pushed himself backwards, like he
was a stone about to be fired in a giant
slingshot . . .

Here goes! thought Blink as he went
hurtling through the air – wings folded
back and beak pointing forward –
travelling far faster than he could ever
normally fly . . . straight towards the
triplets. "Hold on tight to each other!"
he warned them. "Get ready . . . Oof!"

With a watery WHAM! Blink crashed

into Honko, who was already clinging onto Ick and Wick. In the same instant, he started flapping his wings at top speed, propelling the three brothers away from the boat and through the freezing water until they reached a large rock protruding from the foaming ocean – just metres from the edge of the razor-sharp reef!

"Made it," Blink gasped as the empty canoe was lost from sight in a surge of spray and torn to pieces on the jagged coral.

"That was rescue-mongous!" cried Ick, clinging to the rock.

Honko nodded, shivering in the raging water. "And then some."

"Way to go, Blink . . ." Wick gulped. "But I can't keep holding on!"

"Oh, help!" Blink twittered as his claws scraped over the wet stone. "Nor can I!"

"Hang in there!" yelled Teggs as he, Dutch and Damona's Darlings came roaring towards the rock. Their jet-canoes teetered close to the reef, straining against the angry waves as they worked to pull Blink and the stranded triplets to safety. The boats rocked madly and clouds of spray lashed their faces.

Damona waved to Teggs. "We've got Ick and Wick on board!"

"Good work!" Teggs called back. With one last struggle, he and Dutch dragged Blink and Honko into their canoe, then

the cadets steered away from the reef
and made their escape.

"Wonderful!" Spielsaur
was jumping up and
down on the river bank.
"Cammino, Lenswing,
keep filming. What
heroism! What courage!
What a fantastic first
scene!"

"What a disaster!" Damona groaned,
wiping her face. "All that water has
ruined my make-up!"

"That was just *too* close, dudes!" Dutch panted as he finally managed to steer the Daring Dinos' boat back to the jetty. "I thought the jet-canoes were meant to be unsinkable?"

Spielsaur nodded, frowning. "And these robot lifeguards are programmed to never fail."

"They must be f-f-f-faulty," said Wick through chattering teeth.

"But all nine not working . . ." Teggs helped Blink squeeze water from his wings. "What are the odds of that?"

No one had an answer, but Lenswing flapped to the ground and gave a plaintive squawk. Cammino lowered his camera and turned to Spielsaur. "I think she's trying to tell us we should get these guys some warm clothes and a hot drink."

"Sure, Cam – as soon as I've interviewed them!" Spielsaur turned to Teggs and his friends. "Tell the cameras – what were you thinking out there?"

Wick smiled as Netta carried him out of the canoe. "That the water's cold, but my friends are *cool*."

"Saving the lives of others – when it seems no one can help them – is what we're trained for at Astrosaurs Academy," said Damona, fluttering her eyelashes into Cammino's camera.

Dutch mimed being sick, and Teggs and Blink had to hide their smiles.

"Fantastic." Spielsaur smiled. "Kids, that near-disaster was spectacular stuff – but has it put you off appearing in the film?"

"No-way-a-saurus!" Ick shouted, and Teggs and the others all agreed. Lenswing clapped her wings happily.

Spielsaur smiled and pointed to one of the big silver trailers. "Well, in that case, you'd all better climb aboard for a nice warm ride to the next location further round the coast – Battle-Simulation Zone Alpha."

"Wow!" said Teggs, smiling at his friends. "We've never trained at Zone Alpha!"

"Fighting armies of ray-gun-toting training robots sounds a good way to warm up to me!" Blink grinned, leading the charge to the trailer. "Let's go!"

Chapter Four

MECHANICAL MAYHEM

A short while later, Teggs, his friends and the film crew were travelling in their trailers towards Zone Alpha. Stefano Spielsaur had zipped on ahead in his personal supersonic spaceship.

"It's good to
be warm
again," Blink
declared, all
but his beak
invisible beneath
an enormous
white towel.

Teggs nodded happily. "I thought I'd
never dry out."

"But won't it make the film a bit
confusing?" Damona turned to
Cammino. "One minute we're splashing
about in freezing water, the next we're
fighting robots in the jungle!"

"The scenes won't all be shown in
the same order they were filmed,"
Cammino explained. "Stef just wants
to shoot all the tricky action scenes
first while the weather's good. Later
on he'll get you doing your lessons
and all that stuff. Then, he'll take all
the different pieces of film and stick

them together in a way that makes sense."

"I guess he knows what he's doing," said Wick.

"He'd better," said Netta. "I don't want to star in a boring movie!"

"Stef Spielsaur doesn't do 'boring'," Cammino assured her. "He spent the last five years in the Carnivore Sector making mega-documentaries about meat-eaters. Powerful stuff, right, Lenswing?"

Lenswing shivered. "Chirp!"

"Well, I'll let you movie dudes worry how the film turns out," Dutch declared, slurping at a cup of swamp tea. "Me, I'll just stick to the stunts!"

"And there'll be stunts aplenty coming up." Teggs smiled, peering out of the window. "We're about to arrive!"

Battle-Simulation Zone Alpha was an enormous wasteland in the middle of a vast, steamy jungle. The wrecks of buildings blown apart in training exercises lay littered all around.

While Spielsaur worked out his camera angles and the crew set up, Teggs and his fellow cadets changed into special golden battle-armour ready for the shoot.

"This is so exciting!" Netta squealed.

"I know!" Damona pulled on her safety helmet and checked herself in the mirror. "Does my head look big in this?"

"Of course it does, dude," said Dutch cheekily. "You've got the biggest head in the academy!"

Damona thwacked him with her armoured tail. "And you'll have the biggest bruises!"

Then a chunky dinosaur in the red uniform of an astrosaur instructor

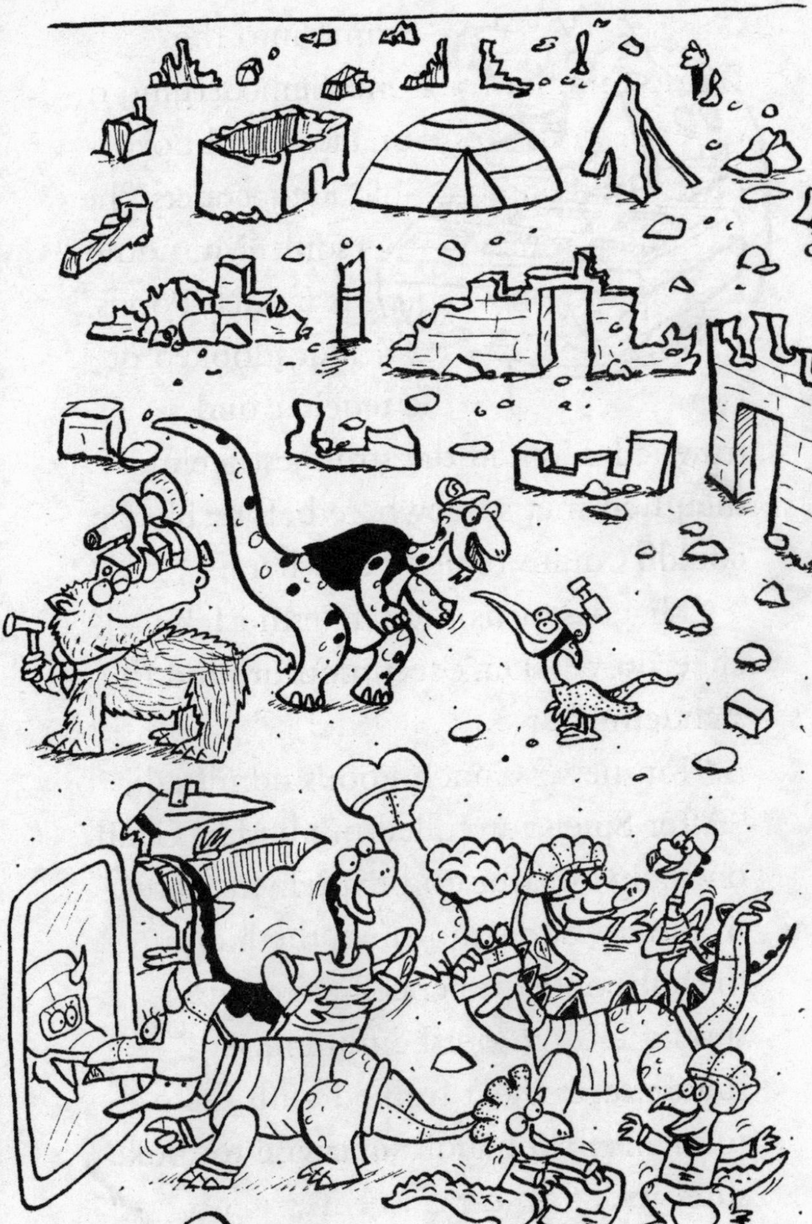

came into the trailer, carrying a big metal box. "Hey, cadets," he said. "My name is Coach Poons." Teggs looked at the teacher and frowned. He had the strangest feeling they had met somewhere before, but he couldn't quite remember when . . .

"Hi-ya-saurus, Coach!" said Ick cheerily. "Haven't seen you around the Academy."

"I'm new," Coach Poons admitted. "After Spielsaur called my buddy Gruff on the way over and explained what went down this morning, the big guy thought an experienced astrosaur should look in on the filming. And since you haven't trained with these robots before, I shall supervise to make sure you stay safe."

He opened the lid of the box and pulled out some ray-guns.

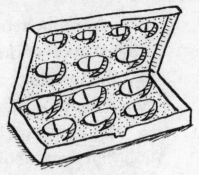

Splatt's eyes lit up. "Stun-pistols!"

"Correct." Poons nodded. "If you zap a training robot three times, it switches itself off and you win. But there are twenty robots in that storehouse – and they're very tough." He handed out the pistols while Cammino and Lenswing set up their cameras. "Better watch out for the robots' electro-blasters, guys. They can give you a nasty shock!"

Teggs felt a thrill of excitement as he held out his hand to Dutch and Blink. "Do we dare take on a bunch of mega-tough robots?"

"WE DARE!" they all cried.

"Is everyone ready?" called Spielsaur.

The cadets came out of the trailer to find the director pointing to a white concrete dome close by.

"The robots are in there. Lenswing, you film from above. Cammino, catch our stars' reactions when they see those bruisers." He smiled at Poons. "OK, Coach, stand by to release the robots. Lights! Camera! ACTION!"

Teggs felt his heart beat faster as he gripped the stun-pistol, bracing himself for a battle. I hope I don't mess up, he thought.

Then the doors to the dome burst open and the training robots rumbled out from inside. They were enormous! Some of them looked like huge metal T. rexes. Others looked like weird, spiky monsters standing on three legs. They all had glowing red eyes and extremely menacing claws . . .

"Uh-oh!" Splatt gulped.

Honko nodded in alarm. "And then some!"

"Let's show them what we're made of!" Damona yelled. She pointed her stun-gun at the nearest robot . . .

And – BLAM! Her gun exploded in a shower of sparks!

"Ow!" Damona yelled, leaping back in alarm – knocking into Ick and Wick as she did so. The two brothers fell into the path of one of the robot 'rexes.

Quickly, they aimed their own pistols. But both of those blew up too! Desperately, Damona tried to help Ick and Wick scramble away. But the metal T. rex fired electro-blasts at the brothers' bottoms. "URRKK!" they yelled, jiggling and dancing in a blur of yellow energy as Damona was blasted clear.

Dutch fired his gun at the attacking robot. The weapon seemed to jump in his hand – and then went up in smoke just as the others' had. He sucked his burned fingers. "What's happening?"

"We can't stop the robots! The guns are useless!" Blink shouted, nearly crashing into Lenswing as another electro-blast whizzed past his beak.

A moment later, Netta was picked up by a mechanical T. rex and hurled down at Honko, squashing him into the ground.

"This is an unfair fight!" Teggs gasped as a spiky robot's fist slammed into his belly-armour and sent him crashing into a ruined building. "Coach Poons, quick – turn them off!"

"I can't!" Poons shouted, hammering at a remote control as a chunk of rubble flew past his head. "Take cover, everyone. The robots are out of control!"

Chapter Five

IN A HOLE!

"Whatever you do, carry on filming!" Spielsaur shouted to his crew. "Cadets, keep fighting. You've got to stop those things!"

"Great idea, dude!" yelled Dutch as a robot grabbed him by the tail and started spinning him around. "Want to tell us how? *Whoaaaaaaaa!*"

Coach Poons ran over to help him, but was hit by an electro-blast. With a groan, he crumpled to the floor. The next second, the robot let go of Dutch's tail. The young diplodocus went flying through the air – *CRASSHHHH* – and right through the windscreen of the nearest trailer.

"Dutch!" Blink squawked, landing on the bonnet. "Are you all right?"

"Things could be worse." Dutch peered out through the broken windscreen, munching on something orange. "I found an old carrot under the driver's seat!"

Ordinarily, such a tasty find would have attracted Teggs's attention. But right now he was too busy yelling and shouting, trying to help Damona lure the training robots away from their fallen friends.

Cammino lowered his camera. "Stef, shouldn't we help the cadets?"

"Keep filming!" Spielsaur ordered. "They must help themselves."

"I thought we were making a documentary," said Netta weakly as Honko dragged her to the shelter of a crumbling wall. "Not a horror film!"

Suddenly, Teggs and Damona jumped. Splatt's head poked out of a hole in the ground nearby. "Look, you two!" he hissed. "I've found a place where we can hide – a big old underground cellar; it must belong to one of the ruins."

Damona looked quickly at Teggs. "Are you thinking what I'm thinking?"

Teggs nodded eagerly. "Those robots are going down!" He shouted across to Dutch. "Can you start up the trailer?"

"Let's see . . ." With Blink's help, Dutch brought the engine roaring into life.

"Get up here, Splatt," said Damona, dodging a robot's punch, and Splatt reluctantly slithered out through the hole. "Help Honko get the others away from the danger zone."

"I'll help too!" Blink flapped over to Coach Poons and dragged him behind a mound of rubble, while Honko hauled Wick away and Splatt helped Ick. A storm of electro-blasts blazed all around them.

"Dutch, be ready to move when we say!" Teggs stood in front of the hole in the ground that Splatt had found. "Damona, we must get those robots' attention . . ."

"Come and get us, rust-brains!" Damona jumped up and down on the spot, pulling rude faces.

"Yeah!" Teggs joined in, stamping hard on the ground and whacking it with his tail. "I've seen tin-openers cleverer than you lot!"

Angrily the robots stamped forward to get Teggs and Damona, red eyes shining.

"Quick!" Teggs yelled, grabbing Damona's hand. The two of them leaped away . . .

Just as the weakened ground above the cellar gave way – and the robots went crashing through it! With an electronic roar, they fell into the dusty darkness, piling on top of each other in confusion . . .

"Now, Dutch!" Damona yelled.

"Here goes!" Dutch hit the accelerator pedal and the trailer roared towards the enormous hole in the ground. With split-seconds to spare, he threw open the driver's door and jumped out, just as the trailer plunged into the hole, smashing down on top of the robots. *KA-KLOOOOOOM!* It exploded with a blinding white flash and a fierce fireball that lit the sky red.

"Wow!" Damona and Teggs said together, staring up at the sight. Then they both realized they were still holding hands, blushed and broke away – to find Coach Poons and their friends climbing dizzily to their feet.

"Is everyone OK?" Teggs asked.

"Head-spin-a-saurus," groaned Ick.

"But we'll live," said Blink. "Way to go, guys!"

Honko, Wick, Splatt and Netta nodded, too exhausted to speak.

Dutch bounded up to Teggs and Damona. "Good work, dudes!"

"You weren't bad yourself." Damona grinned. "For a diplodocus!"

"And . . . cut!" Spielsaur declared as the entire film crew burst into applause. "Who cares if you trashed my trailer? That was spectacular!"

Lenswing flapped down and perched on Cammino's head. "Eep!" she said happily, winking at Teggs.

Teggs smiled back. But he was worried. "First an unsinkable jet-canoe that sinks," he murmured. "Then stun-guns that go wrong and robots that go on a rampage. What's next?"

"For you guys, a good rest," Coach Poons declared. "After all you've been through today, you all deserve a night at Relaxus, the cadet holiday camp." Poons looked over at Spielsaur. "Any objections?"

"No . . . that's fine." The director seemed strangely distracted, looking all about. "I'll send a jet to collect them in the morning. In the meantime, I'll take the crew on ahead to the Dino-Tank Testing Ground in Quarrik, ready for tomorrow's filming."

Blink picked up one of the broken stun-guns and sighed. "I do hope the tanks won't go wrong too!"

"I'll check them myself," Coach Poons promised. "Very closely."

"While *we* check out Relaxus." Netta smiled. "Result!"

It was mid-afternoon when the three teams of astro-cadets arrived at Relaxus, a five-star resort set deep in peaceful rainforest. Luxury log cabins had been quickly booked for everybody, and the battered Baggy Brothers went straight to their rooms for a lie down. But since the sun was still high and shining, Damona's Darlings splashed about in a large Jacuzzi while the Daring Dinos hit the

hammocks that hung between the pool-
side palm trees.

"This is the life!" Dutch declared,
munching on pineapples.

"It certainly is," Blink agreed,
studying two of the exploding guns he
had brought back from Zone Alpha.

Teggs nibbled a giant coconut and
tried to relax. But he kept catching
glimpses of movement out of the corner
of his eye . . .

He had the strangest feeling that he
and his friends were being watched.

Damona bumped a beach ball over to Netta and Splatt and got out of the Jacuzzi. "I'm going to practise my diving," she announced. "I know I'm the only one to get nine out of ten in every swimming class, but I'm sure I can do better . . ."

Dutch rolled his eyes. "When you've finished diving in the pool, go jump in the lake!"

"Jealous!" Damona retorted, climbing the ladder to the top board. She started to bounce. "Just because you're not as graceful as —

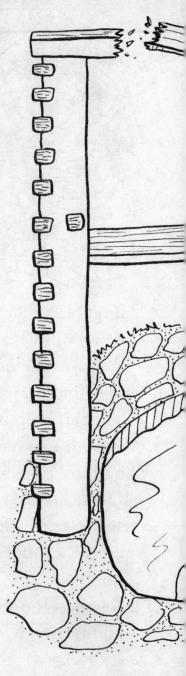

"MEEEEEEEEE!"

Without
warning, the
diving board
shattered into
splinters beneath her! Arms and
legs flailing, Damona fell backwards
into the water – and with a colossal
splash, the ladder and the lower boards
crashed down on top of her . . .

Chapter Six

THE PHANTOM SHOOTER

"Damona!" Teggs charged over to the pool as it foamed and frothed under the massive impact.

Splatt was already pulling bits of debris from the water. "I can't see her!"

Dutch, Blink and Netta slipped and skidded as they frantically helped Teggs and Splatt clear bits of broken board and wrecked ladder.
Then suddenly,
Damona
bobbed up to
the surface,
choking and
spluttering.

Netta wrapped her tail around her friend and pulled her to the side. "Are you OK?"

"I think so," Damona croaked. "It's certainly the first time I've ever been *board* at Astrosaurs Academy! How did the builders get away with such rubbish work?"

"Just take it easy, dude," said Dutch. "You've got a nasty lump there. Oh, no, hang on – that's just your head!" Damona swiped him on the nose with her tail. "Ow!"

"Good aim." Teggs grinned. "I guess you really *are* OK!" For a second, he thought he heard something overhead and the feeling that

they were being watched came back to
him. But when he glanced up, there was
nothing there.

"Guys, look at this!" Blink twittered
urgently. He was perched on a piece
of diving board, floating in the water.
"I don't think the builders are to blame
for what happened . . ."

Leaving Netta and Splatt to look
after Damona, Teggs and Dutch craned
their necks to see.

"Here." Blink tapped his beak against
the edge of the split wood. "If this was a
natural break, it would be rough and
full of splinters."

"I see what you mean," Teggs murmured. "This break is completely smooth. As if it was cut through by a very strong, very precise laser!"

"What are you on about?" said Damona, getting up dizzily.

Dutch studied part of the broken ladder. "Looks like this metal has been cut through in the same way."

"Then someone *wanted* the diving board to collapse into the pool," Teggs realized.

"And guess what . . ." As Netta, Splatt and Damona gathered round, Blink flapped over to his hammock and returned with the two damaged stun-pistols. "See these tiny holes? I think these guns were hit by a laser beam too, even as we held them."

"You could be right, dude," said Dutch, frowning. "I remember the gun seemed to jump in my hand before it exploded . . ."

Teggs stared at the weapons in amazement. Sure enough, a tiny hole had been burned through the metal casings. "The heat of the laser beam must have caused the power packs to explode!"

"And whoever did this could have caused the leak in the Baggy Brothers' jet-canoe," said Netta. "Just by drilling a hole in its bottom!"

"Someone's a very sharp shooter," said Splatt. "But who?"

"They can't have got far." Damona narrowed her eyes. "Let's search for them!"

The cadets split up and looked all around Relaxus. But after hours of searching, they found no

trace of anyone suspicious. The Baggy Brothers were still soundly asleep, and the maids and waiters confirmed that no one else was staying in the resort.

"Our phantom laser shooter must have vanished into the jungle," said Netta, once they had all met up again. "But why are they doing this?"

"Easy," said Splatt. "They're trying to wreck the movie! They've already messed up two big scenes, and now they're trying to put us out of action so we can't film any more."

"But who would want to do that?" Netta wondered.

"The woolly rhino dude told us that Spielsaur spent years recording meat-eaters in the Carnivore Sector, remember?" said Dutch. "Perhaps one of them followed him here?"

Damona gasped. "I just had a nasty thought. What if it's Coach Poons?"

"You could be right," said Blink gravely. "We've only got his word for it that he's friends with Commander Gruff."

"And he was holding the robots' remote-control box at Zone Alpha," Splatt added. "Maybe he got himself blasted on purpose so we wouldn't suspect him."

"He reminds me of someone, but I can't think who." Teggs sighed. "So what are we going to do? I don't know about you lot, but I don't really feel like relaxing any more!"

"I think we should go to the tank range and tell Mr Spielsaur," said Blink. "Right now!"

"But the astro-jet isn't coming to collect us till tomorrow," Netta reminded him.

"I saw a food shuttle land by the kitchens while we were searching." Teggs grinned. "Come on, let's get back into our uniforms – and then see if we can grab a lift and a snack at the same time!"

It took Damona no time at all to sweet-talk the shuttle driver. Once she'd promised to get him Spielsaur's autograph, he was happy to transport the cadets in his cargo hold and drop them at the testing range on Quarrik.

"I hope Ick, Wick and Honko won't

mind being left behind," Blink fretted.
"I know we left them a note to explain
where we've gone, but . . ."

"They could use the rest," Dutch
assured him. "They took a real
pounding from those robots, as well
as getting wiped out in the water."

Teggs nodded. "And hopefully we
can make sure that nothing bad will
happen to them tomorrow!"

The barren landscape was shrouded
in dusk by the time the cadets touched
down on the landing strip. As Teggs
bustled off the shuttle, he saw lights
burning a few hundred metres away.
The film crew had set up a canteen
outside the instructors' control room

 and were eating
their dinner.

"Looks like we got
here just in time!"
Dutch declared,
rubbing his tummy.

Netta stared at him. "But you and Teggs munched through a whole crate of pot plants just before we landed!"

Teggs licked his lips. "Mysteries give us an appetite!"

They made their way over to the canteen, where Cammino welcomed them with some surprise. "Hey, guys! Are you all right?" He scratched his horns. "Didn't you like your rooms?"

"Oh, they were fine," said Damona.
"But the pool was terrible!"

Teggs helped himself to a sneaky mouthful of ferns and looked about for Coach Poons. There was no sign of him.

"We wanted to talk to Mr Spielsaur," said Netta. "Is he here?"

Cammino shook his shaggy head. "He's on his private spaceship, over by the launch pad. Coach Poons wanted to see him too, went over a while ago . . ."

"Did he now," Teggs muttered.

"We'll look for him there," said Blink. "Thanks!"

Teggs and Damona led the way past a long line of parked tanks until they reached the launch pad. Spielsaur's spacecraft was sleek and stylish, like a

giant needle looming darkly above them.

Damona knocked on the door. For several seconds, nothing happened. Then the door whooshed upwards. But no one came to greet them. The corridor beyond was empty save for a single security camera, watching them from the ceiling.

Teggs and his fellow cadets went cautiously inside. Aside from the hum of the lights, the ship was spookily silent.

"Mr Spielsaur?" Teggs called. "Coach Poons, are you there?"

A strangled, desperate chirp echoed from somewhere along the corridor – then cut off.

"That's Lenswing!" yelped Blink. "She must be in trouble."

Splatt gulped hard. "D'you think it's the phantom laser shooter?"

"I don't know." The jagged plates on Teggs's back flushed angry red as he charged away. "But there's only one way to find out!"

Chapter Seven

FILM OF DISASTER

The cadets clattered down the deserted corridors. Teggs flexed his tail, ready for a fight.

The passage ended suddenly at a set of double doors marked VIEWING ROOM. Teggs threw them open and paused in the

doorway, his friends crowding round behind him. The lights had been dimmed. There were rows of chairs on either side and a huge projector screen on one wall.

"It's like a mini-cinema," Blink whispered. "Must be where Mr Spielsaur watches the results of each day's filming."

"Who cares what it is," hissed Damona. "We've got to find that poor little pterosaur!"

But as the cadets crept into the little cinema, the doors slid shut behind them. "Hey!" Dutch banged on the controls beside the doorway. "We're locked in!"

"And look!" Splatt pointed to two huddled figures in the front row. "There's Spielsaur with Coach Poons!"

"All right," said Teggs,

marching over to the coach. "What are you up to, and where's Lenswing? You'd better . . . talk?"

He quickly saw that Coach Poons *couldn't* talk. And neither could Spielsaur. They had both been tied up and gagged!

Damona stared in amazement. "I – I don't understand."

"It's easy," came a nasty, high-pitched screech. "I lured you here . . . and now you are all my prisoners!"

Teggs whirled round. It took him a few moments to notice the little figure in curious headgear standing in front of the cinema screen, wings stretched wide and jaws open in a sneering smile . . .

It was Lenswing – with a laser-gun poking out from her crash-helmet camera!

"Nobody move," she shrieked. "I can zap you wherever you run!"

Blink blinked in amazement. "So you *can* talk!"

"You mean, she can *shout*," Dutch said, holding his ears.

"I can do lots of things," Lenswing rasped. "I can shoot holes in a canoe, disable mechanical lifeguards, scramble a robot remote control or blast stun-pistols from your hands while I'm flying overhead – all thanks to my hot little helmet!"

"So, it wasn't Coach Poons," Teggs breathed. "*You* are the one who's been trying to wreck the film!"

"Did you destroy the diving boards at Relaxus too?" Damona demanded.

"Yes!" Lenswing yelled triumphantly. "I flew out and followed you. What a laugh!"

Dutch scratched his head. "But that wasn't even part of the movie, dude."

"It was a part of *my* movie." Lenswing sniggered. "I'm not only the best ever camera operator – I'm a secret carnivore spy! I joined Spielsaur's crew when he was shooting those documentaries in the Carnivore Sector."

"But you *can't* be a spy!" Splatt protested. "You're so cute and friendly."

"Don't make me sick!" Lenswing sneered. "I *hate* acting sweet and harmless. But it's allowed me to catch all kinds of things on camera . . ."

"What are you up to?" Teggs demanded. "And why have you captured Spielsaur and Coach Poons?"

"Because," said Lenswing, "they found me putting my own little movie together and tried to stop me."

Blink blinked quickly. "What movie?"

Lenswing chuckled. "Since you lot are the unfortunate stars of my little blockbuster, I suppose it's only fair that you should be first to see it!" She

produced a remote control from under one wing. The whirring sound of a projector started up.

Teggs stared at the screen, his jaw dropping in shock.

He saw Ick, Wick and Honko, yelling for help in their sinking jet-canoe. The action cut to Blink whisking them all away – then

banging into the rock with a thud, and
scrabbling to hold on. The next
moment, Damona and Teggs arrived in
their canoes – and the screen cut to a
close-up of Splatt pulling a face as he
nearly fell into the water.

Suddenly, Damona's voice rang out
over the top of the action. "Saving no
one is what we're trained for at
Astrosaurs Academy!"

"I never said that!" cried Damona.
"You've mucked around with my words!"

Splatt cringed at the action on screen.
"The plant-eater public will think they

are being protected by
clumsy idiots . . ."

Lenswing
jumped up and
down with evil
mirth. "You
ain't seen
nothing yet!"

The action cut to the fight with the
training robots. Ick and Wick were
getting blasted in the bottom as
Damona was thrown onto her face.
Netta was hurled into Honko, while in
close-up Blink flapped through the air,
almost banging into Lenswing.
"We . . . are useless!" he cried.

The real Blink squeaked in dismay. "I
said the guns were useless, not us!"

Then the screen showed Damona
climbing the ladder to the diving board.
"I get one out of ten in every swimming
class," she seemed to say – before the
diving board collapsed under her weight.

Seconds later, Teggs and the others were slipping and skidding all over the place as they tried to pull debris from the pool.

"This isn't fair." Damona was close to tears.  "You've put the words and pictures together in a way that makes us all look ridiculous . . ."

"That's right," Lenswing agreed, switching off the projector. "And soon this little film of mine will be shown all over the Jurassic Quadrant to an audience of billions! It will start a terrible scandal . . ."

Blink went pale. "The Academy's reputation will be ruined."

"And ours will be wrecked too!" Damona wailed.

"You're forgetting something, Lenswing," said Teggs. "Cammino and the rest of the film crew all know what really happened. They'll tell everyone the truth."

"Don't think so!" Lenswing's eyes were agleam. "You see, I haven't yet shot the final scene – the one where you bozos accidentally blow up yourselves, and everyone else 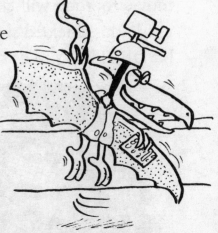 around here, while mucking about in the dino-tanks!"

The cadets stared at each other in horror. "We would never do that!" Splatt spluttered.

"You can't make us," Dutch agreed bravely.

"I don't have to," sneered Lenswing. "At this moment, way above us, a hidden carnivore satellite is moving into position. At my signal, it will fire a missile and blow up the entire testing ground! I shall stay safe, of course, by filming everything from high in the air, and my marvellous movie footage will come to no harm inside this shielded ship – but *you* shall be DESTROYED!"

Chapter Eight

SHOCKS AND SURPRISES

"You haven't got us all in your clutches," Teggs said defiantly. "Ick, Wick and Honko are still safely back at Camp Relaxus."

"I will take care of those bothersome Baggy Brothers once I've taken care of you!" Lenswing lunged forward, grabbed Blink's wing with her pinchy claws and pressed her laser-shooting crash helmet against his head. "Now, grab Spielsaur and Poons and get out to those tanks," she snarled, "or your friend gets it."

"Never mind me," Blink urged his friends. "Stop her!"

Lenswing laughed. "You can't. I'll just fly out of reach and zap you all!"

Dutch turned to Teggs. "What do we do?" he whispered.

"Bide our time," Teggs hissed back. "Come on, guys," he said more loudly. "For now, there's nothing we can do . . ."

Dutch, Netta and Splatt helped Spielsaur and Coach Poons to their feet

and Teggs and Damona led them away, with Lenswing and Blink following close behind. As Teggs left the shelter of Spielsaur's spaceship and stepped out into the dark testing ground, his heart thumped faster and faster. He saw the film crew in the distance innocently enjoying their dinner – if only he could warn them! But if he did, then Lenswing might hurt Blink and who knew how many others. There really seemed no way out . . .

Until suddenly, to his total surprise, Ick, Wick and Honko jumped out from behind the spaceship with a mighty roar! Lenswing leaped into the air in fright, letting go of Blink as she did so.

CRACK! – a second later, Wick's tail struck her right in the belly. With a squawk of dismay, Lenswing went somersaulting backwards – straight into the arms of Honko. He grabbed her, but she wriggled fiercely and pecked him on the chin.

"Look out for her helmet!" Netta cried, pushing Poons and Spielsaur to the ground while Teggs and Dutch lunged for the wicked dino-bird. But Lenswing broke free before he could reach her. She rose into the air and aimed her deadly laser straight at them . . .

"Take *that!*" Damona landed a heavy blow to Lenswing's beak. The screeching spy hovered in midair for a moment, stunned. Then she flopped to the ground. Splatt wrenched off her laser-firing helmet.

"Flapper-strike-a-saurus!" Ick panted.

Wick wiped his brow. "She's out for the count."

"And then some!" Honko beamed.

"Sensational!" cried Cammino, popping up from behind a nearby rock and waving his movie camera. "I was filming the whole thing!"

For a moment, everyone was too stunned to speak.

Then Splatt led the cadets in a whooping cheer. Netta grabbed Ick and kissed him. Damona hugged Honko. Teggs gave Wick a dinosaurly handshake. Dutch did a victory dance with Cammino, while Splatt and Blink quickly untied Spielsaur and Coach Poons.

"Dudes!" Dutch beamed at the triplets. "You completely rock! But how did you get here?"

"I brought them, cadets!" boomed a familiar voice – as Commander Gruff's green, grizzled face poked out from behind Spielsaur's ship! He was grinning, with an unripe banana clamped between his teeth like a cigar. "You see, Spielsaur suspected this film shoot might not go smoothly . . ."

The director nodded. "I made some good contacts in the Carnivore Sector after shooting so many films there.

One of them warned me of a plot to cause trouble here during this filming."

"No wonder you were so grumpy at the start," Damona realized.

"Sorry about that," said Spielsaur. "I was a bit distracted. I didn't know what *sort* of trouble the carnivores would cause."

"So I made sure Spielsaur chose my bravest, toughest, smartest cadets for his movie," Gruff went on. "Cadets who I knew could handle anything."

Teggs understood at last. "So *that's* how we got picked without a proper audition!"

"I didn't like to put you in danger," Gruff went on. "But it was vital we found out what the carnivores were plotting. And of course, you weren't completely on your own . . ."

Coach Poons nodded. "After that marine race trouble, Commander Gruff sent me along to look out for you."

Teggs stared at him. "I can't help feeling we've met before . . ."

Poons grinned. "That's because we have!" He pulled off a mask to reveal the rugged blue features of a different dinosaur beneath . . .

Dutch gasped. "It's Sergeant Snoop, the undercover astrosaur!"

Teggs stared in amazement. "You

helped us a few terms back with that contest carnage at the Megasaur Challenge."

"That's right," Gruff put in. "I was expecting a report from Snoop – or should I say, Coach Poons – this evening. When he didn't call in, I knew there must be trouble."

"So the commander stopped off at Relaxus on the way to check we were all right," said Ick excitedly. "He found your note, woke us up—"

"And you came rushing to our rescue," Damona concluded happily.

"Once they'd asked me to catch the action on camera first," Cammino chimed in.

"It'll make the perfect end to the movie." Spielsaur cheered. "And all our reputations are safe!"

Splatt wiped his scaly brow. "Thank goodness!"

Just then, Lenswing started to stir. "Hold on," Blink twittered. "What are we going to do about her satellite? It's hidden somewhere up above us – armed and dangerous."

Even as he spoke, Lenswing gave a gasp of horror. "Oh, *NO!*" She struggled up from the ground in a sudden panic, and Honko swiftly grabbed her wing.

"Get off, you fool!" she snapped. "When I fell, I must have landed on my remote control – and hit the fire button." She held up the gadget to Gruff. "Look, the countdown's complete. The satellite has launched a mega-missile. It's already on its way to blow us to bits . . . *any minute now!*"

Chapter Nine

EXPLOSIVE STUFF!

"Everyone get into my ship!" yelled Spielsaur. "Lenswing was right – it's got asteroid shielding; it will keep us safe."

"But . . ." Cammino glanced back at the canteen, trembling. "We'll never get the whole film crew inside in time."

"Right, then." Teggs took a deep breath. "We'll just have to take a tank and stop that missile!"

Damona stared at him. "You're crazy!"

"The dino-tanks are armed with dung-bullets, son," Gruff reminded him. "They can't stop a supersonic missile."

"True," said Teggs. "But a laser beam could, and we've got one right here – in Lenswing's camera crash helmet!"

"Of course!" Blink cried. "If we fix it to a tank's gun barrel to keep it steady, and fire the split-second we see the missile . . ."

Dutch nodded. "We might just blow it up before it lands!"

"It's a job for me," Commander Gruff groaned. "But I'm way too big to fit in one of these tanks."

Sergeant Snoop slapped a claw to his forehead. "And I'm not tank-trained . . ."

Teggs gulped. "I almost am!"

"Much as I hate to admit it, Teggs knows even more about tanks than I do," said Damona. She smiled at him encouragingly. "He's the best dinosaur for the job."

"I wish there was another way." Gruff pushed his face up to Teggs's and lowered his voice. "You're a promising cadet. But this is a big risk. Get it wrong, and you'll be blown to pieces."

"I have to try," Teggs argued. "If I don't, innocent dinosaurs will be killed for sure."

"You'll make it, dude," Dutch assured him. "And your ever-lovin' team-mates will back you all the way!"

"Too right!" Blink held out his claw to his friends. "Do we dare to go head-to-head with a mega-missile?"

Teggs and Dutch put their hands on top of his. "WE DARE!"

Then Dutch ran off whooping to fetch a tank, while Blink started studying the laser in Lenswing's helmet.

"All right! The rest of you cadets, inside the spaceship," Gruff boomed. "Snoop, take the spy and go with the others while I supervise things out here – that's an order!"

Snoop saluted Teggs and his team. Then he grabbed Lenswing by the beak and threw her inside the ship. Damona's Darlings and the Baggy

Brothers waved goodbye and plodded sadly after Snoop to safety.

"I'm staying out here with my crew," Spielsaur declared.

"Me too." Cammino nodded behind his camera. "I'm not missing a minute of this drama!"

"I can't order you to go," Gruff grumbled. "Just make sure you don't distract my boys here!"

Seconds later, Dutch came roaring back with a dino-tank. As it screeched to a halt, Blink flapped over with the helmet. Teggs helped him fix it to the end of the long gun barrel while

Dutch scrambled out from inside.

"I'll fly up really high into the sky," said Blink breathlessly, "and signal the moment I see the missile."

Teggs scrambled down inside the tank's cabin. "I'll aim the gun as precisely as I can."

Dutch turned to Teggs. "And I'll hit the hat-laser the moment you're done."

"It's a good plan, cadets," Gruff told them. "Go to it!"

Blink took off into the sky, flapping faster than he'd ever flapped before. Dutch stretched his neck as far as he could, straining to keep the plucky dino-bird in sight. And Teggs wiped his sweaty hands on his uniform and gripped the control lever. Cammino kept filming. Spielsaur and Gruff stood watching in grave silence. Damona and the other cadets stared out of the spaceship windows, hardly daring to breathe.

"How much longer?" Teggs muttered,

sweat pouring down his face, peering
into the gun, his whole body tensed for
action.

"Incoming!" bellowed Blink, waving
his arms frantically. "North-northwest
from sector seven!"

Teggs swung the gun turret round to face sector seven and squinted at the stars in his sights. Sure enough, one was growing larger! He adjusted his aim as the deadly missile streaked towards them . . .

"Fire, Dutch!" he yelled.

Dutch crossed his fingers and let loose the laser beam. A pencil-thin, near-invisible line of energy streaked out from Lenswing's weapon.

Teggs held his breath . . .

And the missile exploded in midair,
like a huge fiery flower blossoming above
the testing ground!

Cammino cheered
wildly. "They did it!"

Gruff laughed so
loudly he dropped
his banana! "I never
doubted them
for a second."

The shock waves sent Blink plunging back down to earth – where luckily he was caught by a speechless Spielsaur.

"Looks like you caught a falling *star*, Mr Director!" said Damona cheekily, rushing outside with Splatt, Netta and the triplets close behind her. She grabbed Blink and perched him on her

head-frill, while Splatt and Netta raised
Teggs onto their shoulders and the
Baggy Brothers did the same for Dutch.

"Three cheers for the Daring Dinos!"
Snoop proclaimed, dragging out a
handcuffed Lenswing. "They're *all* stars."

"They certainly are," Spielsaur
agreed. "I wasn't expecting this
documentary to turn into
quite such a drama – but
when it's shown on
prime-time TV, the entire
Jurassic Quadrant will be
talking about it!"

Cammino turned
to Lenswing. "Don't
worry about missing
out, 'old buddy'," he
said coldly. "I'm
sure you can
watch it on
the space-
prison TV!"

"But no one will ever watch Lenswing's rotten movie," said Splatt, throwing black shreds of film over the pterosaur spy. "I'm afraid the critics *tore it to pieces!*"

Snoop grinned. "Marauding meat-eaters will think twice about invading the Vegetarian Sector when they see how tough and brave plant-eaters can be."

Gruff nodded. "You cadets will inspire thousands more young dinosaurs to come to Astrosaurs Academy and train to be the best."

"Great!" said Blink.

"Just so long as they don't eat all the food in the canteen," Teggs joked.

"Well, since you'll be guests of honour at the grand movie premiere I'm planning," said Spielsaur, "I'll provide the biggest banquet you've ever seen!"

"Imagine," said Damona, nearly swooning, "posing on a red carpet made of poppies . . ."

Dutch was drooling.

"*Eating* a red carpet made of poppies!"

"It's all well and good being film stars," said Blink. "But I can't wait till we're proper astrosaurs travelling *among* the stars."

"Right!" Teggs grinned around at his friends. "You can keep your lights and your camera – just give me the ACTION!"

THE END

The cadets of
Astrosaurs Academy
will return in
CHRISTMAS CRISIS!

Astrosaurs
THE SUN-SNATCHERS
STEVE COLE

Teggs is no ordinary
dinosaur – he's an
ASTROSAUR!
Captain of the
amazing spaceship DSS *Sauropod*,
he goes on dangerous missions and
fights evil – along with his faithful
crew, Gipsy, Arx and Iggy!

A world of woolly rhinos is
in desperate peril – one of their three
suns has gone missing! Racing to the
rescue, Teggs and his team must fight
a gigantic star-swallowing menace
before theother two suns get snatched
away. And all the time, other
dangers are drawing closer . . .

ISBN: 978 1 862 30254 9

ASTROSAURS ACADEMY
CONTEST CARNAGE!
STEVE COLE

Young Teggs stegosaur is a pupil at **ASTROSAURS ACADEMY** – where dinosaurs train to be **ASTROSAURS!** With his best friends Blink and Dutch beside him, amazing adventures and far-out-fun are never far away!

Teggs and his fellow astro-cadets can't wait to compete in a brand new sports tournament on the Academy's doorstep – the Megasaur Challenge! But when several athletes are injured in a number of nutty "accidents", the contest is plunged into chaos. Suspecting foul play, Teggs investigates. But will he survive long enough to learn the terrifying truth?

ISBN: 978 1 862 30555 7

THE PIRATE MOO-TINY
by Steve Cole

OX MARKS THE SPOT!

Genius cow Professor McMoo
and his trusty sidekicks, Pat and
Bo, are star agents of the C.I.A.
– short for COWS IN ACTION! They travel
through time, fighting evil bulls from the future
and keeping history on the right track . . .

In 1978, robotic danger HAUNTS
the seven seas . . . Posing as a pirate, a
TER-MOO-NATOR is capturing ships in
the Caribbean. But why? And what terrible
treasure is he hiding on SPOOKY Udderdoom
Island? McMoo, Pat and Bo set sail on a big,
BUCCANEERING adventure to find answers
before pirate BULLS takes over the world . . .

It's time for action. COWS IN ACTION

ISBN: 978 1 862 30541 0